Curious George®

Makes Maple Syrup

Adaptation by C. A. Krones
Based on the TV series teleplay written by Chuck Tately

Houghton Mifflin Harcourt Publishing Company
Boston   New York

For information about permission to reproduce selections from this book, write to Permissions, Houghton Mifflin Harcourt Publishing Company, 215 Park Avenue South, New York, New York 10003.

ISBN: 978-0-544-10494-5 paper-over-board
ISBN: 978-0-544-03252-1 paperback
Design by Afsoon Razavi
www.hmhbooks.com
Printed in China
SCP 10 9 8 7 6 5 4 3 2 1
4500440220

George loved mornings in the country. Sunday was his favorite morning of all, because Sunday was pancake day! Today, the man with the yellow hat was teaching George how to make pancakes.

"When they start to get bubbly it means they're ready to flip!" his friend said.
George flipped each pancake as it was ready—one, two, three!

George started pouring a lot of syrup on his pancakes.
"Go easy on that maple syrup, George. It doesn't grow on trees," the man
said. Then he thought for a moment and said, "Well, in a way, it does!"

George was confused. He imagined picking bottles of syrup off the trees like apples. The man explained that the syrup doesn't actually grow on the trees. It comes from inside the trees! All you have to do is tap them.

George had poured all of the syrup on his pancakes. Now there was no syrup left for his friend. But George had an idea. There were plenty of trees outside. All he had to do was tap them!

George put on his coat and went outside. There were many trees on the Renkinses' farm. He tapped on each tree like he was knocking on a door.

George's friends Allie and Mr. Renkins came over to see what he was doing.
"George, why are you knocking on that tree?" asked Allie. George showed
them the syrup bottle.
"Are you looking for syrup?" Mr. Renkins asked.

"First, you've got to tap the tree to get its sap," Mr. Renkins explained. "That doesn't mean knock on it. You have to hammer the tap into the tree. Then you can collect the sap in a bucket. Like this." Mr. Renkins demonstrated.

Mr. Renkins had an extra bucket to spare, so George and Allie could collect their own sap. George was excited. He could cover mountains of pancakes with a whole bucket of maple syrup!

Mr. Renkins explained that to find a maple tree, you have to know the characteristics to look for.

Maple trees have gray bark with deep ridges, and they grow their own special leaves. The leaves have five points—just like on the bottle of syrup!

After Mr. Renkins showed them how to tap a maple tree, George and Allie were ready to tap one on their own! But finding the right tree wasn't easy. After spotting one that had gray bark with deep ridges and five-pointed leaves, they knew they had found the right kind of tree!

The sap dripped. And dripped. George and Allie waited. And . . . they waited.
They must have tapped the slowest tree on the farm.
Finally, George's bucket was full. Now they just needed to make more pancakes!

Back at the house, Allie and George surprised their friend with a pancake breakfast and their new syrup. But when the man poured the syrup on his pancakes, it didn't taste like maple syrup at all!!

What had gone wrong? They went back to Mr. Renkins for answers. He explained that sap becomes syrup only after it's boiled down. Luckily, he could help them boil the sap into syrup at the sugar shack!

"It takes a while to boil, but if you leave it too long it can bubble over and burn," Mr. Renkins warned. "I'm going to go check on the cows. You two keep an eye on the sap."

George and Allie watched the sap and waited for it to boil. Mr. Renkins was right. It was taking a very long time, and they were getting tired!

Suddenly, the sap started to boil over. George tried to fan the sap with pancakes to cool it down. But the butter on the pancakes slipped into the pan. The butter smoothed out the sap and kept it from boiling over! Mr. Renkins returned and said that the butter had stopped the sap from burning. Now it had finally turned into syrup.

With the help of Allie and Mr. Renkins, George had made a bottle of his very own maple syrup!

The next Sunday, George made pancakes for his friend and poured his homemade maple syrup on them. "Thanks, George," said the man. "This is the best Sunday morning syrup I've ever had!"

How to Make a Leaf Log

A log is like a journal. It's a place to write down observations about nature. You can write words in it or even draw pictures of what you see in nature! Mr. Renkins knew which trees to tap for sap because he could identify the characteristics, or traits, of a maple tree. He knew that they have a particular kind of leaf that has five points. You can make these kinds of observations about trees and their leaves too!

Ask an adult to take you on a nature walk. Don't forget your leaf log and a pencil.

What do you see? What kind of bark do the trees have? Describe them in your log. Write about what the leaf looks like. What characteristics does the leaf have? How many points? What color is it?

Pick out a few special leaves to bring home with you. You can easily make a leaf impression in your leaf log by following these simple steps.

Tools you will need:

- Colored pencils or crayons
- Paper in your leaf log
- Some of your favorite leaves!

Directions:

1. Place your favorite leaf underneath the page you would like to draw it on.
2. Make sure your piece of paper is over the leaf in the spot where you want it in your journal.
3. Use your colored pencil or crayon to lightly color on the paper over the leaf. Do you see shape of the leaf coming through?
4. You can use different colors to imitate the changing colors of the leaves!
5. Check out a book from the library to help you identify the types of trees your leaves are from.

Plant or Animal?

George learned that maple syrup comes from maple trees. Lots of things we eat and drink come from nature. Look at each of the pictures below and guess which of these yummy items come from plants and which ones come from animals.